Barrab.

CW00496699

Bassoon
Scales & Arpeggios

from 2018

ABRSM Grades 1–5

Contents

First published in 2017 by ABRSM (Publishing) Ltd, a wholly owned subsidiary of ABRSM
© 2017 by The Associated Board of the Royal Schools of Music
Unauthorized photocopying is illegal

Music origination by Julia Bovee
Cover by Kate Benjamin & Andy Potts
Printed in England by Halstan & Co. Ltd, Amersham, Bucks., on materials from sustainable sources

Grade 1

SCALES

from memory
tongued *and* slurred

one octave   ♩ = 50

F major

G major

E minor
natural

or

E minor
melodic

or

E minor
harmonic

ARPEGGIOS

from memory
tongued *and* slurred

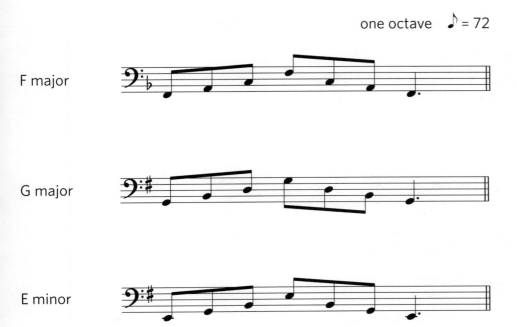

Grade 2

SCALES

from memory
tongued *and* slurred

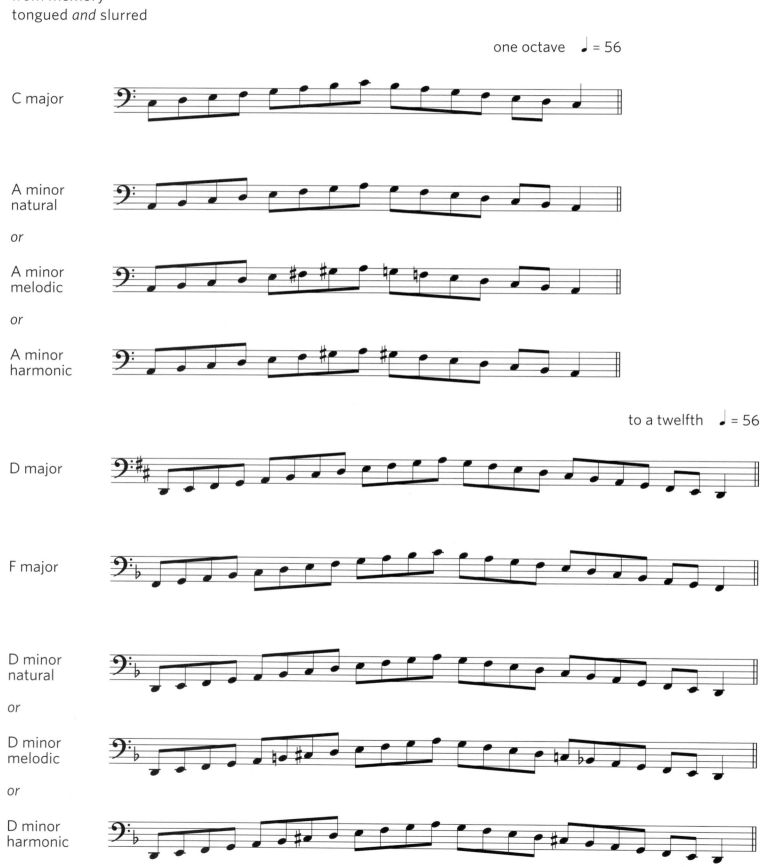

one octave ♩ = 56

C major

A minor natural

or

A minor melodic

or

A minor harmonic

to a twelfth ♩ = 56

D major

F major

D minor natural

or

D minor melodic

or

D minor harmonic

ARPEGGIOS

from memory
tongued *and* slurred

one octave   ♪ = 84

C major

A minor

to a twelfth   ♪ = 84

D major

F major

D minor

Grade 3

SCALES

from memory
tongued *and* slurred

to a twelfth   ♩ = 63

G major

A major

B♭ major

E minor
melodic

or

E minor
harmonic

A minor
melodic

or

A minor
harmonic

two octaves   ♩ = 63

C major

D minor
melodic

or

D minor
harmonic

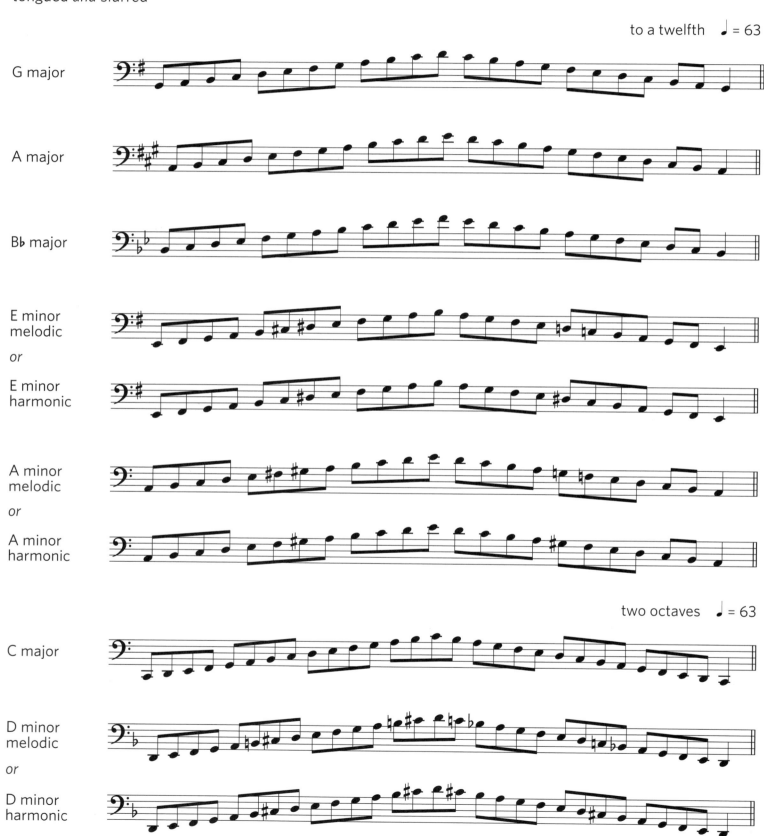

ARPEGGIOS

from memory
tongued *and* slurred

to a twelfth ♪ = 96

G major

A major

B♭ major

E minor

A minor

two octaves ♪ = 96

C major

D minor

CHROMATIC SCALE

from memory
tongued *and* slurred

one octave ♩ = 63

starting
on G

Grade 4

SCALES

from memory
tongued *and* slurred

two octaves ♩ = 72

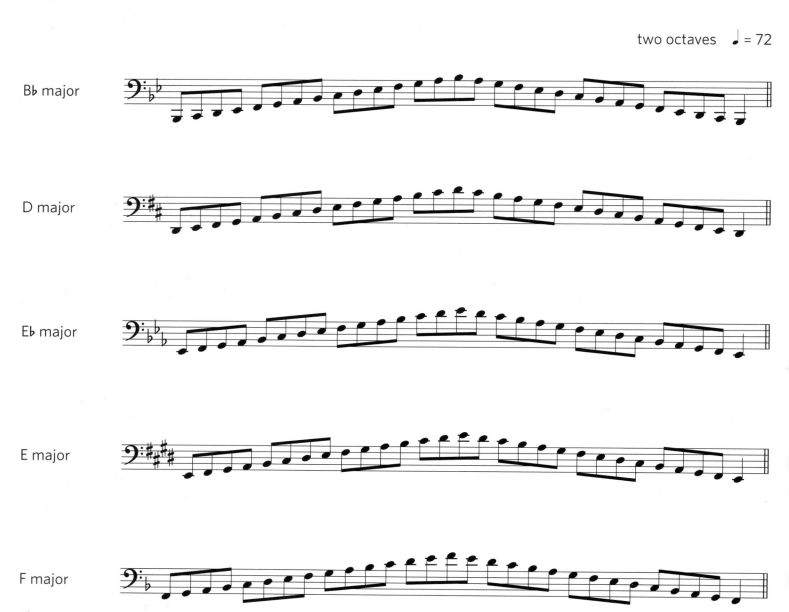

Bb major

D major

Eb major

E major

F major

B minor
melodic

or

B minor
harmonic

C minor
melodic

or

C minor
harmonic

E minor
melodic

or

E minor
harmonic

G minor
melodic

or

G minor
harmonic

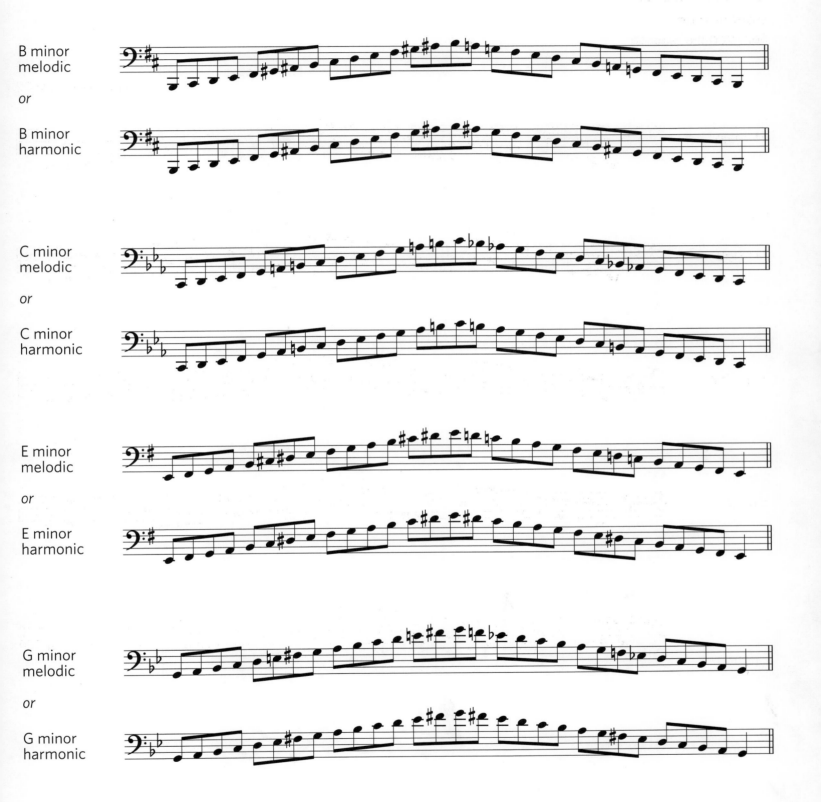

Grade 4

ARPEGGIOS

from memory
tongued *and* slurred

two octaves ♪ = 108

Bb major

D major

Eb major

E major

F major

B minor

C minor

E minor

G minor

DOMINANT SEVENTH

from memory
resolving on the tonic
tongued *and* slurred

two octaves   ♩ = 54

in the
key of C

CHROMATIC SCALE

from memory
tongued *and* slurred

two octaves   ♩ = 72

starting
on F

Grade 5

SCALES

from memory
tongued *and* slurred

two octaves   ♩ = 84

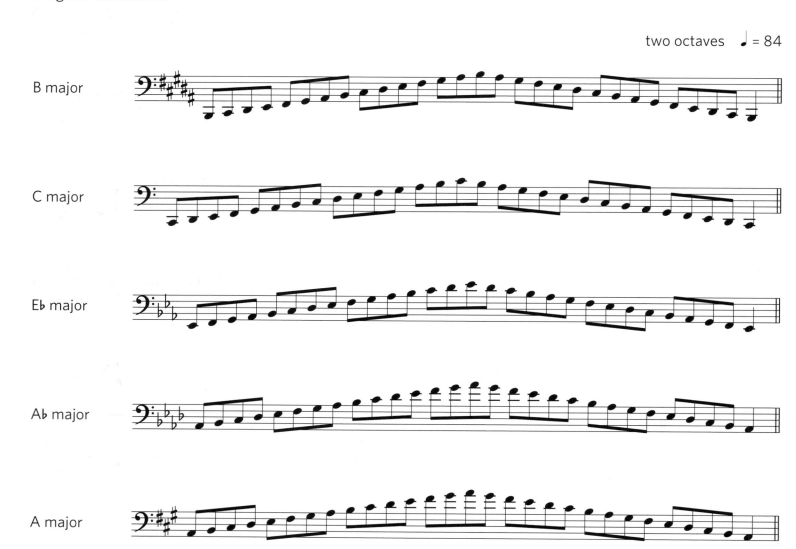

B major

C major

E♭ major

A♭ major

A major

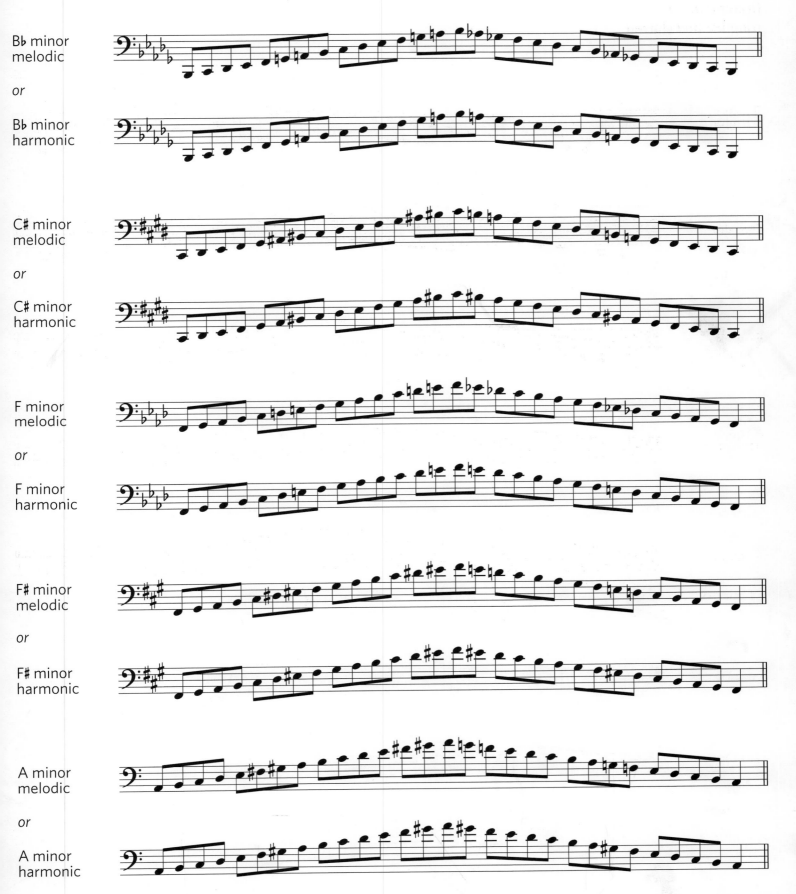

Bb minor melodic

or

Bb minor harmonic

C# minor melodic

or

C# minor harmonic

F minor melodic

or

F minor harmonic

F# minor melodic

or

F# minor harmonic

A minor melodic

or

A minor harmonic

Grade 5

ARPEGGIOS

from memory
tongued *and* slurred

two octaves   ♪ = 126

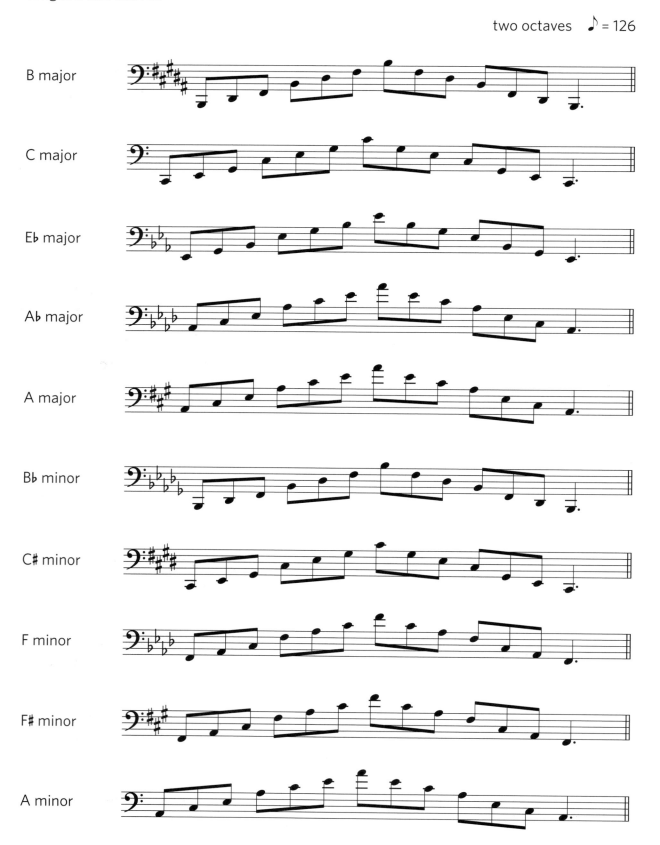

DOMINANT SEVENTHS

from memory
resolving on the tonic
tongued *and* slurred

two octaves   ♩ = 63

in the
key of F

in the
key of D

DIMINISHED SEVENTH

from memory
tongued *and* slurred

two octaves   ♩ = 63

starting
on F

For practical purposes, the diminished seventh is notated using some enharmonic equivalents.

CHROMATIC SCALES

from memory
tongued *and* slurred

two octaves   ♩ = 84

starting
on C

starting
on A♭

23/04/2024

Scales: think about :
    1. Starting once and only once!
    2. Crescendo to top
    3. even note lengths
    4. push through heels

all scales need to be at the same speed

B major lower octave needs work

All Slurred arpeggios - clean fingers, don't hit every note on way up +
down.

next week: all majors, major arps + dom 7ths

high Gs. bigger half hole !